Wing & Arrow

ALSO BY PIPER CJ

No Other Gods

The Deer and the Dragon

The Fox and the Falcon

The Night and Its Moon

The Night and Its Moon

The Sun and Its Shade

The Gloom Between Stars

The Dawn and Its Light

Accompanying *The Night and Its Moon* Novellas:

A Night Without Whispers

Wing and Arrow

A Year of Tea and Honey

Crown and Crumble

Villains

A Chill in the Flame

Fern's School for Wayward Fae

The Graveyard Gift

Wing & Arrow

zaccai's story

PIPER CJ

To those of us with hearts that don't fit in a box—
All relationships are real and valid…
unless someone in your polycule tries to get you killed

CONTENTS

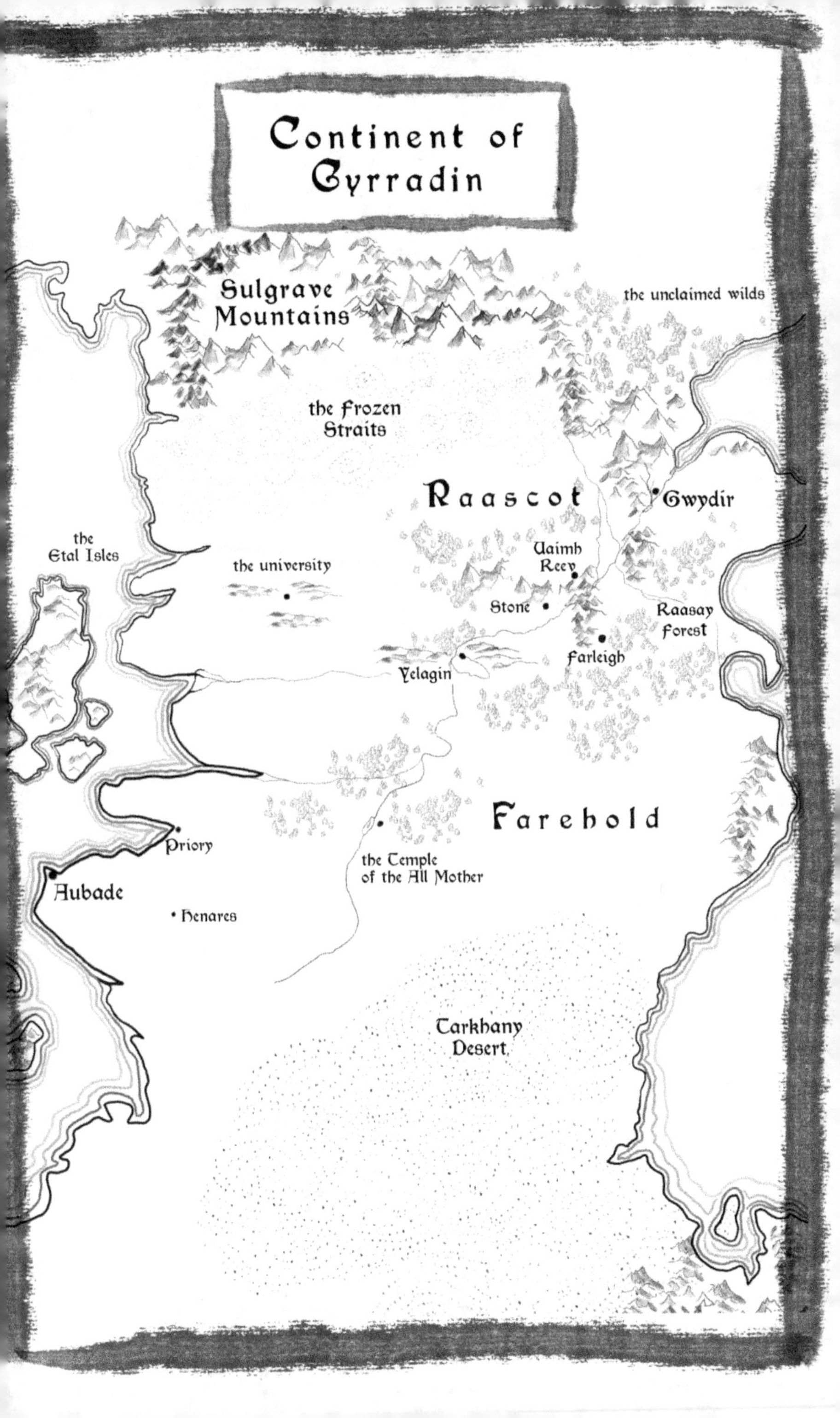

Continent of Cyrradin

Sulgrave Mountains

the unclaimed wilds

the Frozen Straits

Raascot

Gwydir

the Etal Isles

the university

Uaimh Reev

Stone

Raasay Forest

Farleigh

Yelagin

Farehold

Priory

the Temple of the All Mother

Aubade

Henares

Tarkhany Desert

PART ONE
VALOR

"Again?"

The young woman grinned up at Zaccai from beneath the cloud of sweat and tangled hair. The only light in the tent came from the fires that crackled throughout the training camp. Her skin shimmered even in the dim, orange lantern light. He'd been thrilled when the two of them had been assigned to the same camp to oversee the new troops, and rightfully so. One could endure any of life's unpleasantries with someone lovely in their bed.

"I thought fae were supposed to have more stamina than that?" the woman teased.

"Goddess, Bri," Zaccai panted, slipping a hand beneath her back and flipping her until she was below him. "Are you sure you aren't part fae?"

Briar slipped her hands beneath his wings, digging her fingernails into his back and drawing deep, red lines to emphasize her enthusiasm. Her legs encircled his hips, flexing and wrapping around his waist to guide him in once again.

His mouth moved against her neck, lips and tongue at first,

followed by a hard bite that elicited a delicious gasp from her throat. Her entire body tightened in pleasure as he dragged his teeth along her skin. He could be gentle when the occasion called for it. He could be tender, and slow, and intimate. He could bring flowers or write letters or trace his hands along the fingers that held his. But those were not the sorts of things she wanted. No, Briar was a voracious creature, and goddess be damned if she didn't bring out the deepest, most primal parts of him.

"Don't stop," she moaned.

He obliged. With slow, deep, rhythmic precision, he rammed himself into her, savoring the build of her moans until she was so close that he could practically taste her climax. Without warning, he stilled within her. Her eyes shot open, feral and demanding.

"Hey!" Briar panted at what had been denied.

Zaccai slid out and flipped her in a fluid motion, yanking her hips up to meet his as he rose to his knees. He didn't miss her appreciative grin. She dropped her chest low, bracing herself as he filled every inch of her. Gooseflesh rippled down her spine as each nerve tingled and swam with tantalizing domination. He wasn't sure how many times Briar could climax in one night before she unraveled, but if she was determined to find out, he was more than happy to oblige.

The sensation that pulsed through him was so much more than lust. He looked at the arch of her back, the firm muscle of her thighs, the strength in her posture, her thirst for life, and drowned in an ocean of respect and awe.

Perhaps now was not the time to think such thoughts, but against the slapping of flesh, the hard grind of teeth as their passion rose, he couldn't help it. He had no control over his heart.

Goddess, she was something.

He would love her if she would let him. He'd fuck her and taste her and then hold her, hear her dreams, listen to her wishes and wants and woes. If she'd fall, he'd catch her. But when she'd showed up at his door, she'd been clear about who she was and what she wanted, which, unfortunately, had only made her all the more loveable. Briar had been well-named. She was bloom and beauty and thorns in a splendid, inseparable package. She couldn't stop him from falling for her, but he could honor her wishes and never press her for more. This was her dance to lead.

He closed the part of his mind that thought of flowers and promises and focused on the way his fingers dimpled into her soft flesh, savoring every sound, every thrust, every burst of ecstasy that shot through him. The explosion that followed was worth every bit of his attention. He collapsed beside her as she finished, wishing he could capture the sound she made when she came. It was absolute music.

"I don't know if anyone's ever told you this." She rolled onto her side and spoke between gasps. "But you're not terrible in bed."

"Not terrible." He chuckled breathlessly. "Please put that on my tombstone."

Her white teeth glinted against what remained of the orange glow late into the night as she smiled at him. He melted into her like little more than butter over warm bread, body and soul utterly drained. She dragged her fingers along his bare skin in a familiar way that told him she was preparing to leave. She was one move away from lifting his hands off her body and slipping from from his tent.

"Sleep here," Zaccai said, tightening his hold. He knew she wouldn't, but it didn't stop him from asking.

"You know, I rarely wish I was fae? Except when I'm with you."

His heart squeezed at her words. "Oh?"

She nodded. "You smell like scotch, and fire and autumn leaves. I know it's a fae thing, and I love it and hate it in equal proportion. Do you know the sort of effect you have on humans? What do I smell like, flesh and sweat?" She laughed lightly.

His heart sank, but he did his best to conceal the disappointment. Perhaps he'd been getting ahead of himself to think she might be wishing for immortality when she was with him. It was a fruitless wish. He shook his head, pressing his mouth to her hair. "You wash your hair in a chamomile soap, don't you? I smell it every time we're together. Chamomile and rebellion."

"You can't smell rebellion," she argued.

"So you say."

Time stretched between them as they drank in the perfume of scotch and chamomile and sweat and sex. After a long moment, Briar broke their post-glow reverie. She smiled and rolled to look at him. "Do you know Wren?"

He frowned at the change in conversation. "From your unit? I've seen the man in passing, but you're the only archer I spend time with."

"Have you heard anything about Wren making rank? I hear he's up for captain."

Zaccai sucked on his teeth as he considered the question. "Is that what you want to talk about right now? The archery unit?"

"It's relevant."

Zaccai pushed a puff of air through his nose that might have been a laugh. "Goddess, Briar, relevant because... Are you trying to fuck him before he's your superior? That's a dangerous game, Lieutenant."

She ran her fingers along his chest. "Calling me by my rank in bed, Commander? You're a poet. Now answer the question."

"With the skirmish at the border, I think a few slots have opened up." Zaccai frowned at his choice of words. Death was nothing to joke about. No one joined the military without understanding the intrinsic risks. It was part of what he liked so much about Briar. Fully human, her life was short and fragile, yet she'd dedicated herself to taking every moment by the balls. Whether fucking or fighting, she believed with her whole heart that when one's existence was short, no moment should be wasted. Zaccai retrained his thoughts to answer her question.

"I think he's due for a promotion. I can ask Gad next time I see him."

"I still can't believe you refer to him like that."

"Gadriel?" He laughed. "We're practically family. Do you want me to call him 'The General'?" Zaccai flexed his fingers around the word to emphasize his entertainment. The men had known one another since infancy. Military born and bred, they'd been raised as brothers in every way but blood. Once in a while, he'd hear one of the new troops whisper about Gadriel's nepotism title, but it was the sort of ignorant comment one could only say if they didn't know him. No one in Raascot was more suited to lead. Still, their professional ranks had never stolen from their friendship.

"No, no, don't ask our general. Don't bother him with that. I was just wondering what you knew."

Zaccai shrugged. "I'm less invested in what the other units are up to. Bri, if this is about getting laid, I don't need to tell you that you shouldn't be sleeping with anyone in your flight. I happen to know a fellow officer who's both available and would love to keep you in his bed."

"There are only six officers in this camp! You know how big the dating pool would be if I could fraternize with the whole battalion? There are at least two hundred and fifty enlisted troops at this camp, and I haven't so much as looked at a single one because I'm a pillar of virtue and professionalism. Now, be a good sport."

"Yes, the troops are so lucky they don't have a predatory officer," he mocked, eyeing her still-naked form. She was stunning by fae and human standards alike. Her skin was a richer shade of smoky amber than most in Raascot, her inky hair almost always in a single braid down her back, save for when she was in bed. She didn't have the fragile, delicate features so narrowly lauded in ballads. She wore her strength from the square of her jaw to the muscular set of her arms and legs. Despite his propensity for humor, he knew that if she were a less principled individual, she'd have no trouble circumventing the rules. Any number of genders would trip over themselves for a chance to pass time with her, for her beauty, her wit, her bravery alone. She would, of course, be held accountable and tried accordingly. It wouldn't have been wise to ally herself with the commander in charge of espionage if she had anything to hide.

But she never did. She wore both her heart and her intentions on her sleeve.

Briar rolled so as to force Zaccai onto his back, perching herself lightly on top of him. She rested her head against the bare skin of his chest, listening to his heart. The young lieutenant continued tracing lines from his chest down to the deviation of his abdominals as she spoke. "I have every intention of staying in your bed, Cai. But if the two of us already have incredible sex, imagine how much better it could be if we add a third. That's just good math."

He considered the idea. "Wren, you say?"

She nodded. "What do you think? His eyes are quite pretty. They're almost a shade of crimson."

"No one has red eyes."

"He does. They're a gold-brown, I suppose, but there's a garnet undercurrent to them. It's really something. You'll see what I mean. He has a neat ability too. It's almost as unique as his eye color."

"And what ability is that?"

"It's something like empathy, but I didn't really understand it. He didn't do a great job explaining it, but maybe that's what made it more interesting. You're the spymaster, why don't you do a little digging and find out for me?"

Zaccai considered what he knew of the man. "I've done worse." His brows lifted as he flitted through his memories. "Wren seems quiet, but I guess I don't know much about his character. Our units don't interact often."

"Do you think he'd be amenable?"

"To your unquenchable appetite?" Zaccai grabbed the back of her head and forced her forehead to his lips. "Who wouldn't be?"

At the show of affection, Briar took her cue to leave. Zaccai pursed his lips to keep himself from sighing as she stood and began to redress.

"There's nothing I can say to make you stay here, is there?"

She shook her head. "I'm trying to curry favor with my captain-to-be, aren't I? Can't be waking up with my bunk empty."

He tsked. "It's a bad idea."

"So you've said."

"If there's even a chance of him becoming your unit's superior—"

"Then we'd better make it quick, don't you think?" Briar slipped into her shoes and bent to give him a parting kiss. She'd intended for it to be brief, but Zaccai held her neck, hovering above her lips for a moment longer until she slowed down, truly absorbing his kiss.

✦

Zaccai looked at the sun and cursed the time. Of all nights to lose track of time, of course, it had to be tonight. He'd had high hopes for the special operations unit when they'd been recommended, but as the hours stretched from sunrise to sunset, he'd reached the conclusion that none of the recruits were cut out for his logistics team. No one came into the world inherently good at any job or skill. These troops had been recommended based on their fae powers and predispositions for shielding, dampening, vocal casting, and abilities that might make them compatible for reconnaissance efforts. Whoever had compiled the list had failed to take into account their demeanor, tenacity, and competence.

He made no effort to conceal his displeasure with their performance as he wrapped up the exercise.

"Commander, I'd really like another chance. I think if you gave me—" One of the troops was doing her best to apologize as she caught pace with him. He'd heard the excuses ten thousand times.

Zaccai pursed his lips to keep from saying something he'd regret. After exhaling, he said, "Today wasn't your best day. That's okay. But no one is special for being born with an innate ability."

"Will I be able to apply again? Will any of us—"

"Yes." The word was more biting than he'd intended, but given who was waiting for him back at the tent, he was feeling exceptionally impatient. "But don't come to me unless you've put in the work. Tell the others."

"Thank you, Commander." She tried to jog to keep up with him, but stopped when he waved her away. His day had stretched from four hours into ten, and he didn't have an extra minute to spare. Zaccai was already hesitant about involving another officer in their endeavors, but arriving hours after Wren and Briar had been drinking would be another wet blanket over the evening. No one enjoyed being the only sober party at an event.

Zaccai's tent had been the obvious choice. If they'd been in Gwydir, there would have been any number of locations available to them. As long as they remained in the encampment, he'd be the only one high ranking enough to offer them the privacy for Briar's appetite.

It was nearly sundown after he'd showered and crossed the camp. He heard a burble of laughter from beyond the tent's flaps as he approached, and couldn't explain the spike of nerves he felt. He'd been with men before, whether in group experiences or alone. The fae life was long, and anyone who refused to experience what it had to offer was in for a cold, empty immortality. Something else drove his cortisol as silvery anxiety snaked through him. Maybe it was an urge to protect Briar from something she might regret if she woke up to Wren as the archers' commanding officer. Maybe it was nothing. He had a nagging feeling that it might be something else entirely.

Zaccai put on a smile before knocking, his fist making perfunctory, near-muted taps against the canvas before he began to untie the knots that held them shut.

"Cai!" Briar's voice called long before he'd finished with the ropes. At the sound of his name, his smile became genuine before he finished unraveling the ties.

His eyes went first to her, then to the newcomer. The fae he could only assume to be Wren stood somewhat awkwardly from where he'd been relaxing, whiskey in hand.

"Commander," Wren said woodenly, wings folding behind him.

"Please." Zaccai waved it away. "Call me Cai."

Briar was already on her feet, pouring a drink for Zaccai and refilling the other two glasses. She pressed the cup into his right hand, then the crystal decanter into his left. "You're at least three drinks behind. Do us the honor?" Briar tilted the container slightly. Ever the good sport, Zaccai complied.

He took three large gulps of the dark, burning liquid. She grinned, and Wren visibly relaxed at the commander's informality. Wren returned to his chair while Briar took a seat on the bed. She stretched her hand for Zaccai, who slid in easily beside her. He knew better than to look too possessive. This was not a night for arms around backs or hands around waists.

"Wren," he said, raising his glass, "tell me, when you were a child, what was your worst fear?"

Wren blinked several times. "What?"

Briar shrugged. "Mine was thunderstorms. I think it's

because our neighbor could speak to the weather, so I suspected any rumble of the clouds was a direct response to her moods. I walked on eggshells around the woman."

Zaccai smiled at the story. He'd heard it before. It had struck him how little he knew of the human experience, even within Raascot and its extreme attempts at integration.

"I suppose I was afraid of demons," Wren said. "There are so many that seem nearly human or fae, don't you think? Beseul, ag'imni, sustron...they're all..."

"Almost people?" Zaccai offered.

Wren nodded. "Why do you think that is?"

Zaccai shrugged. "I couldn't guess. But I agree: it makes them worse. I'd take a vageth over a beseul any day. Have you ever seen one?"

Wren nodded slowly. "Yes, once. It was why I joined the military. My father and I came across a beseul when we were hiking. It was one of my youngest memories. We didn't move for hours. His abilities are useful around the hearth and home, but could do very little if he needed to protect his son from a demon."

"Goddess." Briar rolled her eyes. "Leave it to you to pick the most morose topic! Okay, I'm next. Wed, bed, behead. The general, the king, and the All Mother."

Zaccai narrowed his eyes. "You're going to hell for that one."

She grinned. "I think I'd marry the All Mother and bed our general. I wouldn't mind a deity for a spouse."

Zaccai shook his head. "Killing our king, then? You're going to hell *and* prison."

Briar's delight swelled. "What happens in the tent stays in the tent. Wren? What about you?"

Wren's jaw dropped. "You're asking me between the goddess, the monarch, and the head of our military? In front of our Spymaster? You're trying to get me in trouble."

Zaccai chuckled into his whiskey. "The sooner you catch on to how much trouble she is, the better off you'll be."

"Fine." Briar's sound was one of mock exasperation. "Wren, you come up with a question, will you?"

He held the amber liquid near his mouth and examined it for a minute, then looked at the others in the tent. Wren tossed the liquor back and made a loud, swallowing sound before asking, "Would you rather?"

Briar's eyebrows lifted appreciatively. "Go on?"

Zaccai passed him the half-full decanter of whiskey. Wren poured two fingers of the liquid into his glass before sucking up his courage. "Would you rather give or receive?"

Zaccai smiled. "Give."

Briar beamed. "Receive."

✦

Brick by brick, a number of core memories had shaped the foundation on which Zaccai was built. Happy memories, like the time his mother gifted him with a tricolored puppy that covered him in licks and kisses filled him with pure, innocent joy. The tragedies of holding his first troop on the battlefield after his man had fallen to an arrow, or the day his father had told him to be the man of the house as he'd left for a new life in Farehold, had cracked him and reformed him in pained, shadowed shapes. The experience of hot, almond pastries for the first time, the green, wild sound of the fiddle saturating him with an unheard song, the first time he saw a spotted fawn in the wild were all joyous occasions that buried themselves into his heart. The sound Briar made as he held her, his mouth against hers, lips parted for her gasps while he filled her, absorbing her moan as she was entered by another, rooted itself in an entirely new bank of memories. Purity and depravity, authenticity and experience, indulgence and chaos wove themselves into her musical notes of pleasure, the way her spine curved, the way she clutched him as if he were the only raft in a stormy sea as she was overcome with sensation, it had been formative in a way he'd never be able to put into words.

Zaccai was no stranger to sex. He'd fucked. He'd made love. He'd tried, and sampled, and experimented. And then, there was this. A moment so intoxicating, he wished he could bottle it and sip it like wine.

Perhaps knowing they were temporary was part of their pleasure.

Nothing transcendent can last forever.

PART TWO
RECONNAISSANCE

"That's much better," Zaccai said appreciatively, and he meant it. The troops had worked hard after their last dreadfully disappointing meeting. He'd made them wait nearly a month of independent exercises before the few bold enough to continue at their task scheduled a second meeting to apply for his team. He wasn't ready to promise any titles or positions within his logistics team, but at least he had a few prospects on whom he could keep an eye.

"Is there anything else we can do, Commander?" the same ambitious fae asked. "I could stay late—"

"No!" He cleared his throat, knowing he sounded far too eager to dismiss his duties. In his defense, he always stayed much later than expected. He should have dismissed them hours ago. If he allowed the new recruits to keep him a moment longer, he'd be cutting off his ear to spite his face. After all, the human life was as short as the fae life was long. He wasn't willing to waste precious moments while he felt Briar's mortality ticking away. It didn't matter that they'd only known each other for five years, or had been sleeping together for three. He loved his job. He loved his king, his country, and the military. But his position in Raascot would always be here. Briar, on the other hand...

It was the quickest shower of his life, but he couldn't very well show up from a day of training unbathed. He hadn't even waited for the water to get warm before the soap, suds, and arctic splashes from the showers had finished. Zaccai toweled off and calmed himself slightly before entering the tent.

Wren's face brightened every bit as much as Briar's upon his arrival. Zaccai grinned. "Why is it I always feel like I'm late to my own party?"

Briar rolled her eyes—a signature move for the spirited lieutenant. "Your party? Please. As if we all don't know who's the star of the show."

He bit his lip against his smirk as he and Wren exchanged looks. Briar certainly stole the spotlight. Perhaps a human life didn't feel so short if you had two immortal beings worshipping your every inch. If life was a game, she'd won.

"Sit, sit." Briar motioned.

He slid next to Wren, slipping his arm around the lieutenant's shoulders while Briar busied herself with something or other.

Zaccai smiled. "Should I ask you how work was? Or is today one of the days where you'd prefer to pretend we aren't in a training camp?"

Wren caught his eyes for a moment, and he caught the same chips of ruby Briar had once mentioned. The man had whiskey-colored eyes, but a reddish glow emanated from within the crown of his irises. Zaccai could have sworn the same crimson hint spread from Wren's neck, though he wasn't entirely sure what caused it. They'd played their games of pleasure and release for the better part of a month. He admitted to himself that he'd been wrong to question Wren's involvement. Briar had impeccable taste in men, after all.

Wren had been nervous on their first encounter, but only in

the way that anyone might be on their first time with all new experiences. He was in the safe company of generous, patient teachers. Briar's enthusiasm made up for a multitude of blunders. By their third, then fourth, then fifth time, there was little in the way of confidence. Their chemistry as a trio built on each meeting.

"It was nothing special." Wren looked into his dark liquor, unwilling to meet Zaccai's gaze.

Zaccai made a face and took the glass from Wren's hand, setting it to the side. They were beyond the point of needing liquid courage. As if protesting the motion, Wren snatched the cup the moment it touched the ground, tossing back its remnants. Zaccai tried to catch Briar with his curious eye for answers, but she remained occupied with her alternate tasks, back to the men.

Briar finally turned from where she'd been occupying herself and procured a fist with two pieces of straw. She offered her closed fist and a wide smile.

"Whoever draws the long straw gets the truth, and whoever draws the short gets the dare."

"To be clear..." Zaccai arched a brow. "You're playing a children's game? This is how you want to spend your night?"

"Yes," she said confidently. "And I hope that one day everyone is old enough to realize they wasted years being too big or too good or too proper for any small joy this stupid world has to offer. Children have the right idea. Don't question the simplicity. Play the game."

Amused, Zaccai quirked a quizzical brow. "And what do you get?"

"I'm the game maker. I get to play god."

"I'm pulling rank on that one. Get a third straw and reshuffle."

She muttered something about how in the tent, there was no rank, but returned to cut another stalk. With three pieces in her left hand, she wiggled the fingers of her right and said,

"Now, on my mark, we'll all pick at the same time, okay? Short gets truth, long gets dare. Ready, set..."

They plucked in unison.

Wren and Briar each came up with a straw roughly the length of a knuckle, while Zaccai's was the length of a finger. They looked at their game maker expectantly.

"Excellent," she purred. "Wren?" she asked. "Have you ever been with a man alone?"

Wren's face turned a near-purple shade as he shook his head slightly. Zaccai did his best not to smile, knowing it would be disrespectful to react with a positive or negative. It had been Wren's truth to share, not his to react.

She grinned wickedly. "Zaccai, do you know where I'm going with your dare?"

He looked at his straw, then up at hers. "I think I get to ask you your truth first."

"Oh?" She raised a brow.

He nodded. "Tell me the truth, oh great game master. How long have you been orchestrating this?"

Briar's smile flickered slightly. She bit her thumb as she looked from one to the other, then began to unbutton her top. She maintained eye contact as she slipped it off her shoulders, then slid the tips of her fingers into her pants, ready to play as she eyed them. "It seems like you already know the answer. Now, are you ready for your dare?"

Zaccai set down his piece of straw and watched Wren, studying the blush of his neck for hints at his emotion. He reached out a finger and squeezed the man's shoulders until Wren looked at him.

"It's just a game," Zaccai said. "No one has to do anything they don't want to. You're under no—"

The column of Wren's throat worked. Zaccai saw Wren choke on his nerves the instant before the man's mouth touched his own. He was loosely aware of the scrape of fingers, the tug of fabric, the flare of wings, and the bruising grip of strong hands. Briar made her pleasure known without lifting a finger to intervene, enjoying every touch, every kiss, every suction and grab and swallow. The growls, the rapture, the flesh and sex and indulgence that swelled within the tent was intoxicating. She remained to the side, but spectating was far from her final form. Zaccai was quite certain Briar finished once, then twice, then a third time long before they were done with each other. Feathers, pleasure, skin, lust, and escape filled the midnight hours.

At least for one, buzzed, blissful night, nothing else mattered.

PART THREE
DEPLOYMENT

"Cai?"

Zaccai's head whipped at the unexpected voice. He saw the face of his troops fall as the archery unit's most stunning human lieutenant approached. He'd had a suspicion that a few of the soldiers who'd been coming to him for prospective logistics had less than altruistic motives, but their expressions gave them away.

Briar had never come to see him on the job. The archery unit was on the far side of the camp, and their paths had no reason to cross. She'd also never referred to him so informally in front of their troops. She was an officer in her own right, even if he outranked her. She knew better than to use such an affectionate term in front of his retinue.

He motioned for his troops to continue their practice as he stepped off to meet her, face creased with worry. His hand found the small of her back as he ushered her away from prying eyes and ears. Her human ears may not have allowed her the supernatural predisposition for eavesdropping, but she'd spent enough of her life around fae to fully understand how great his gift for dampening was. He cast a barrier over them, protecting their sound from carrying. He didn't ask what was wrong. He trusted her judgment enough to know that she came with a reason.

"I'm sorry for interrupting," she began.

"Don't be," he said, and he meant it.

"I know you run late with your troops, and I'll be gone by the time your shift ends. I wanted to say goodbye."

A ringing hummed through his body. It wasn't just the high-pitched resonance of a bell, but the uncomfortable vibrations through his very capillaries. He knew enough of dispatches and movements to understand that she wasn't being sent back to Gwydir.

"You're going to the border?"

She looked away. "We're not going to fight. Not yet, anyway. It's an intelligence mission—"

"I'm intelligence!" he said, temper flaring. He hadn't meant to flex his hold on her arm so hard as he spoke. He wasn't angry with her—not in the slightest. He relaxed his grip. "This should be a logistics effort. The archers shouldn't go to the border over their squabble. I'll talk to Gad—"

"It was his order."

A muscle feathered in Zaccai's jaw. "No, Gadriel hasn't even been to the camp. I would have heard. I would—"

"He sent word. We're just there for backup at a distance. It won't be a long mission. I'm just meant to provide coverage at range. I'll be fine."

"Is Wren going with you?" he asked hopefully.

She shook her head. "He's finally getting that promotion."

Zaccai's heart dropped into his stomach. "Your captain should be with you. If he's making rank, he has all the more reason—"

Briar freed her arm. "It's because only a few of us are going, and it isn't that serious. This isn't the entire archery unit. This isn't an offensive effort. A handful are going to provide coverage, that's all. Wren is staying to oversee the archers at camp as the remaining officer. His promotion is too fresh for him to be qualified for much more than that. We need the major with us at the border, not a newly minted captain. I'll be back in a week or two. I'll be fine."

Zaccai's forehead creased with worry. "Briar, you're—"

"Human?"

He looked away.

They were well aware that some of his troops eyed their meeting curiously, but she took his hand in her own. Their words, at the very least, were safe under his net of dampening. "I'd be human whether or not I went. I'd be human if I stayed perfectly safe and lived to be ninety-nine, never going anywhere or doing anything. Then what? You'll stay young and strong and perfect, and I'll have never lived? This is the life I chose for a reason, Cai. I know you respect that. Don't change now."

He looked into her eyes, tumbling into their bottomless depths. He felt every moment they'd shared. Every word he wished he'd said, every moment he'd ached to hold her, every second he'd wished she'd let him love her swelled within him.

"I want to kiss you goodbye," he said.

He wasn't shocked to see the familiar expression as she rolled her eyes. "That is offensive, professionally disrespectful, and also deeply insulting, as it implies I won't return."

"It implies I care about you."

She squeezed his hand. "Show me you care about me when I get back. I'll make an extensive, graphic list of exactly how I'd like to be cared for."

The corner of his lip tugged up in a smile that didn't meet his eyes.

"While I'm gone, have fun with Wren, okay? He really likes you."

"Briar—"

She huffed. "This isn't about me. You two get along well.

Don't pretend you don't like him back. And please believe me when I tell you that the two of you are as hot as sin together. I'll consider it a personal favor if I can let my imagination run wild with what you're doing in my absence. Just save room for me when I return."

She gave him a parting squeeze before she stepped away, breaking the dampening cone he'd cast around them. The world's sounds crashed in, surrounding him in the meaningless burble of newly enlisted hopefuls as Briar walked away. Zaccai was loosely conscious of the exercises that continued as his troops trained, but couldn't tear his eyes from Briar and visions of an unprotected human alone at the border.

The exercises went on. He was a professional and knew how to focus, but his mind was leagues from the task at hand.

Zaccai sent everyone home hours early that night in an attempt to intercept the major of the archers. While he had no direct authority in their unit, he outranked them. He knew the major would hold an audience if he demanded it. When it came to throwing weight around, it didn't hurt that everyone in the camp knew that the Spymaster and Raascot's highest ranking general were friends. Zaccai pushed through the tents in an effort to reach the archery unit when he spotted a flash of her hair.

Briar was in her full hardened leathers, issuing orders as the commanding officer to the enlisted archers below her. He caught a glimpse of the major from the corner of his eye, and all thoughts of interceding left him. He deflated as he watched her in her element. This was where she wanted to be. This was the life she chose. This was the adrenaline, the risk, the authority, the fun and fear and joy that she wanted from her life. It would be so much more than selfish to intervene.

Zaccai inhaled sharply as he took a step back, ensuring that she wouldn't see him. He didn't go so far as to cast his dampening. He was adept enough at sleuthing without needing to call upon his natural abilities. He'd seen her shoot a bow. He'd seen her lead the soldiers below her. More importantly, he'd witnessed her spirit, her fight, her strength, and the way in which she twisted every drop out of life.

He shouldn't worry about her, but he did. Not because she wasn't capable, but because he didn't know if he was. She'd lived a full and happy life before she met him, and she'd undoubtedly live a full and happy life without him.

He wasn't certain he could say the same.

Zaccai was halfway toward his tent when Wren fell into step with him.

"I'm sorry," was all Wren said.

Zaccai nodded, not looking at the man. "Me too."

Zaccai caught Gadriel's eye the moment the general stepped into the buttery glow of the campfire. Orange outlined the edges of his friend's wingspan, gilding him like a dark-winged angel of lore. He'd missed his friend. He wasn't too proud to rush into their embrace, wings flapping once, then folding behind him as he crushed Gadriel in a hug.

"Gad! What the hell are you doing here?"

Gadriel squeezed him in return before holding him at arm's length. It wasn't quite a party, but the training camp had a relatively jovial atmosphere as troops poured ale and gathered into various war stories, competitive games, and miscellaneous unwinding after hours. Those on patrol cast side-long glances soaked in jealousy at the respite offered to everyone who'd been on the day shift.

"Let me get you a pitcher!" Zaccai grinned, breaking free from their hug long enough to fetch two lukewarm pints for each of them. "Do you know anyone who can freeze things?"

"Yes!" Gadriel held up a finger as he shouted to a fae with auburn hair. He introduced her as one of his sergeants, and she made a wisecrack about how her gift was more than a party trick before chilling their beer. If Zaccai didn't know better, he could have sworn the woman flipped a vulgar finger to match her smile as she flitted away. Given his own propensity for friendliness within his ranks, perhaps he needed to reflect on the compiling evidence that Raascot's military was far too lax.

Gadriel lifted his drink in a toast. The general's eyes crinkled with his smile. "Are you keeping them in order for me?"

Zaccai made a face His tone caught somewhere between an amicable jest and a bitter edge. "As if I have any say in the matter? Are you responsible for the garbage being sent my way? I'm two weeks away from firing the reconnaissance efforts and making the spy network a one-man job."

Gadriel laughed. "I wish I were to blame. It's possible that we're passing task assignments too far down the chain of command. I'll talk to the colonel and see why you're being sent untrained fae."

"If it's the recruiter—"

"It's always the recruiter."

They shared a chuckle at that, imagining the bright-eyed fae being promised a position with the spymaster [CD3] simply because they'd displayed an aptitude for something or other associated with espionage.

"I've been a little focused on holding down the fort in Gwydir while Ceres goes on his ambassador missions," Gadriel said. There was a blue tone to his voice that implied he was leaving something unsaid. Zaccai waited for Gadriel to elaborate, but he didn't. He finished his beer before his face shifted to something a little more business-like. "Has Ceres been here? He's been hard to pin down lately."

Zaccai drank deeply, then frowned unhelpfully. "I think I'd remember if the training field was graced with our king's presence. How are things in Gwydir?"

Gadriel shrugged. "Uneventful, which is how we like them. You'll have to remind me to tell you the story of how we got one of our troops to discover his ability to crack the earth."

"Where?" Zaccai grimaced, remembering just how unpleasant combat training had been for he and Gadriel alike. It was a rite of passage for all fae to endure before being assigned to their unit. Fortunately, neither he nor Gadriel had caused structural damage while unlocking their power.

"The crack? It's just outside of the facility. I think we'll keep it. Turn it into a moat."

The conversation dwindled as Gadriel smiled at his own joke.

"Other than that, there have been reports of a few too many demons, but we've written Uaimh Reev on the matter. Unholy creatures are their specialty. As long as we can keep tabs on military efforts between the kingdoms, I think they'll more or less handle the rest."

Zaccai's face fell as he looked into the dredges of his beer. He rose, then took the time to fetch two new glasses. This time they had to make do with warm ale.

"What is it?"

Zaccai looked up at his friend. "I have to ask: Why would you send an archery team for reconnaissance efforts? I won't question your rationale, Gad. You're the general. I just feel like this is something that should have been handled by logistics."

Gadriel matched his frown, brows furrowing. "I'm not sure what you're talking about."

Zaccai sighed. "It's nothing. A friend of mine...a small batch from the archery unit was sent to the border. I know it's just a territorial dispute, but we've lost a number of lives over it. I expected my team to go before an offensive unit."

Gadriel's mouth turned down. "I haven't dispatched anyone new to the border."

Zaccai's face twisted into puzzlement. He studied the face in front of him as both a friend and a general. "Do you know where your archers are now?"

The general paused for a moment before his face lit. "Yes!" he said at last. "A small team from this camp volunteered their support. I didn't realize it was exclusively an archery team, but they weren't dispatched. They put themselves forward. No general would turn down willing coverage."

Zaccai's fingers tensed around his glass. He fought the twitch in his lip as a flash of anger shot through him. Of course Briar would send herself to the front lines. Zaccai looked into the fire while he let his emotions flicker, matching the reds and yellows and oranges of betrayal, confusion, pain, and truth. Gadriel went on to talk about his life in Gwydir, a drinking friend he'd made in the capital, adjustments to life in Raascot following his parents' departure, and anecdotes regarding sharing a roof with the increasingly aloof King Ceres.

"Do you think that's part of why your parents left?" Zaccai asked. He did his best to stay engaged in the conversation while forcing down acidic feelings for an archer who'd rather play fast and loose with her life. He had a friend who wanted to be with him, and that was what mattered.

Gadriel cocked a brow, though from the number of discarded pitchers at their feet, it was clear neither of them would be responsible for critical thinking that night.

"Their son and their nephew are ruling the kingdom," he went on. "They want you both to grow into your own. Would it be a disservice if they stayed?"

Gadriel made a dismissive gesture, though the glazed look on his eyes betrayed a lack of care that came more from alcohol's pleasant cocoon than from anything anchored in emotion. "Perhaps after a few centuries, I'll also need to do something no one's done before. Humans say life is short, and it's why they do the unimaginable to make every moment count. I say life is terribly long, and so for the same reason, we have to make it as interesting as possible."

Zaccai continued looking into the fire as Gadriel spoke. His eyes snagged up on a shape across the flame while his friend finished his words of wisdom, catching on Wren's form. The newly minted captain raised a finger from his pint in acknowledgment. Zaccai held Wren's eyes for a moment too long.

"Gad?"

"Hmm?" The general drained his what remained of the lukewarm pitcher, question echoing through the dredges of his beer. His buzz had distracted him for quite some time.

"I'd love to stay and chat, but I have first-hand knowledge as to how none of us could kill you if we tried. I'm quite confident you're fine on your own. Would you forgive me if I call it a night? There's something I need to do."

Gadriel looked into the bottom of his glass, then to Zaccai, then to where his eyes had caught across the ever-dancing firelight. Gadriel made an appreciative face. "Far be it from me to keep you. I'll see you back in Gwydir when you've finalized your team."

Zaccai clapped him on the shoulder as he stood, still holding Wren's eye. He jerked his chin once toward his tent and the new captain of the archers understood the gesture. Zaccai caught the flare of wings from the opposite side of the camp as the man stood, knowing Wren was following.

✦

"I've never—"

"You have," Zaccai responded with steadying reassurance.

"Briar was always here—"

"Does she need to be?" Zaccai asked, anger still pricking at the knowledge that she'd willingly sent herself to the border. He'd be lying if he said spite and ale hadn't driven him to this moment, no matter how much he'd enjoyed his time with Wren. His anger and disillusionment burned hotter than outright lust, but the flame scalded regardless of its source.

Wren's shoulders lifted as his chest expanded. He exhaled slowly, summoning his bravery as he squared off with the commander. The happy sounds of fire, games, and music blazed from beyond the walls of the tent, sheltering them within the privacy of their shadows. Zaccai was of a slightly larger build and greater wingspan, but they were roughly the same height, with various shades of night in their hair and eyes alike, save for the ever-present ruby stitches possessed by Wren alone.

They remained locked in a standoff, illuminated only by the dim, filtered light of fire through the canvas. Each stared for a moment too long before Wren responded, "No, she doesn't."

PART FOUR
HOMECOMING

Zaccai usually woke with the sunrise, but stirred a little earlier than usual.

"Tea?"

He offered a drowsy smile as he sat up, still undressed from the night before. He accepted the cup from Wren and drank deeply. He would have appreciated the strong breakfast brew, an herbal tea, even a glass of cold water from anyone in the morning. There was something so thoughtful about the person who shared your bed waking before you to ensure your first experience with the day was pleasant. This wasn't the first time Wren had fallen asleep in his bed, nor was it was first time he'd been offered a drink well before sunrise. Maybe it had been Briar's unwillingness to stay the night, or his lingering bitterness over her lie at what had driven her to the frontlines, but each morning, the coffee was sweeter. Each night, the warmth of the body beside him filled him with the soothing balm his aching heart needed. Perhaps he hadn't seen that papercut after papercut, her minor rejections had compiled into a deep, throbbing wound. It wasn't until someone arrived to soothe it that he'd realized how much he'd been willing to withstand in the name of hope.

"You're cutting it close to firing time, don't you think?" Zaccai asked.

Wren was unbothered. "I'm always there on time. It wouldn't serve me well to be late within my first month of making rank."

"The new recruits fall apart pretty quickly without a strong hand. I'll deny it if you tell them I said so." He smirked into his mug. "You should get going before they see you leaving my tent."

Wren laughed quietly, his amusement restrained enough to respect the purple hour of dawn. "As if leaving the spymaster's tent at dawn wouldn't gain me higher regard. Maybe they'd start to see me for who I am."

Zaccai did his best to contain his smile. It felt good to be appreciated.

Wren wasn't a morning kisser, which was fine. Their kisses had been secondary to the rest of their activities, particularly given how resentment had been the foundation on which their house was built. Zaccai's spite had dissipated as the weeks had passed, though hate had certainly been at the wheel the first few times they'd fucked. He was leagues away from considering any of their entanglements to be lovemaking, but at the very least, acrimony had been chiseled into consistency and appreciation. Release, companionship, and recognition weren't qualities one should take for granted. As much as he resented Briar, her taste in men truly was impeccable. Wren was quiet, yes, but he was considerate, strong, handsome as hell, and unrelenting in his willingness to give. Briar had always been the taker. It was a relief from a burden he hadn't realized he'd shouldered to finally be on the receiving end.

Wren slipped out of the tent while the violets of first lights faded into the pale, pink gradients of morning. Zaccai spent the morning enjoying his strong, dark tea while he got ready in the quiet solitude of life before the camp was awake.

He headed to his training grounds early, cup slowly cooling in his hands against the chilly morning air. He liked the brisk, pastel hours before the rest of the world was awake. Zaccai put down the silty, bitter leaves of tea that remained at the bottom of his cup and began to set up his station before the ever-dithering number of his troops arrived. He hadn't named an official number of enlistees who could or could not join his reconnaissance forces, but he was prone to err on the side of caution. If it hadn't been for the tenacities of those under his wing, he may have given up altogether. Their fortitude proved more than his own intuition ever had, and for that he was grateful. One of his best qualities was his willingness to be proven wrong.

"Commander?" A voice came from behind him.

He controlled his face, smoothing out the lines of his flinch before he turned toward the troop who'd hounded him since their first session. He didn't want to insult her by assuming she was a girl with a crush—but she was. Perhaps she had a crush on military life, or on the concept of espionage, or maybe on Zaccai himself. The who, what, and why didn't matter. Her infatuation with one element or the other had made her incessant questions unbearable.

Zaccai pursed his lips as he turned to look at the overeager soldier.

"You have two hours before you have to report," he said.

"I know," she agreed quickly. "This isn't about work—"

He bristled at that. "If it's not about work, you shouldn't be here. It's not appropriate to—"

"Goddess, commander, no, I'm not hitting on you." Her eyes widened. "I'm so sorry, I respect that boundary. It's part of what makes you a good leader. Goddess, I'm making this worse. I sound like a kiss-ass. I—"

His brows gathered in frustration. "It would be great if you could spit it out."

"The archery unit is back," she said. "I was up and heading to the showers when they arrived. I just saw you leave for the day, and since we still have a few hours before training... I'm sorry, I shouldn't have come. I didn't mean to make you think. Oh, fuck—"

His eyes widened. He motioned with his hands. "No, no, I'm sorry for snapping," and he was. He'd assumed the worst and regretted it. "The archery team?" he repeated, and he knew she understood his question.

"No fatalities, sir. I know your friend—"

"Thank you." He squeezed her shoulder briefly in what was perhaps a too-friendly gesture before jogging off into the late salmon colors of morning toward the shadow outlines of their distant tents. His prospective team had witnessed his goodbye to the archer weeks prior. Perhaps his troops knew more than they were meant to, but for the moment, any irritation evaporated. All he could think of was how badly he'd wanted Briar to fall asleep beside him. He'd craved the sound she'd made when she was happy. He wanted to bathe in the fullness she felt for life, taking every risk, experiencing every joy. He was so excited to hear she was alive, it took him a minute for him to remember that his bitterness hadn't gone anywhere. Still, its presence was secondary to his need to see her living body for himself.

Zaccai was so focused on the distant shape of her bunker that he nearly crashed into her. If it hadn't been for his wings and preternatural speed, he would have knocked her to the ground. Instead, his arms broke their impact with an all-encompassing embrace that shocked them both. He swept her against him as his wings unfurled in a powerful back-beat to keep them on their feet to counteract his momentum. He hadn't meant to hug her. He'd been so surprised to find her in his arms that he hadn't been able to contain himself.

"Cai!" Briar gasped through the hug.

He dropped her to her feet. "You evil bitch!"

Her jaw dropped in shocked, laughing surprise. "Well, fuck you too! What the hell!"

Something about the exchange of obscenities relaxed the tension between them more than he could explain. He embraced her again, then his fingers gripped her hard enough that she cried out in genuine pain. "Cai!"

"I can't decide if I should kiss you or kill you," he said into her hair.

"Do I get a vote?" Briar asked as she pushed out of the hug. She forced him to an arm's length and examined him.

Zaccai raked a hand through his hair. His fingers stopped, bunched at his crown, holding a handful of his own hair in frustration. "You volunteered to go to the border," was all he could say.

Her face twisted, brows furrowed. "What are you talking about?"

"Your mission to the goddess damn border dispute! You reckless fucking—"

"I didn't volunteer, Zaccai."

"You did!" He pressed, agitation overtaking his joy. "I spoke with Gadriel—"

"The general?"

He rolled his eyes. "Yes, I talked to 'the general' about your dispatch! It was a volunteer mission! The way you came to say goodbye? Goddess, Briar, I knew you were named for thorns, but you shouldn't be this hard to hold onto." Zaccai's voice broke off in a mingle of frustration and sorrow. In his haste to run to her tent, he hadn't considered how infuriated their reunion might make him. She'd lied to him. It had been an insult upon the injury he'd done his best to respect—he'd honored her wishes to be nothing more because he'd taken her at her word. She'd always been honest with him about who she was and what she wanted. This had angered him more than anything. Either she'd change course and altered her core character, or she'd never been honest to begin with, and he'd fooled himself to believe he ever truly known her.

"Cai, what are you talking about?"

His hand dropped from his hair and hung limply at his side. "I'm sorry. It's so early. I know you just got back. This shouldn't be a conversation for the twilight hour. I was so surprised that you'd arrived, I didn't think—"

"I genuinely don't know what you're talking about."

His brows lowered as he eyed her.

She shook her head, reiterating, "Our unit was volunteered. I didn't willingly go to the border."

"Bri—"

She looked at him with extreme suspicion as she picked through her next words. "I did not want to leave. I didn't want to go to the border. I'm fine though, by the way. Thanks for asking. Yes, it was traumatic. Farehold is full of soulless barbarians, and I can't be convinced otherwise."

He blinked against the tumultuous wave of emotions crashing through him. "You didn't volunteer?"

"You're a terrible spymaster. I've told you more than once now! Do you listen? How did you get promoted to commander of reconnaissance if you're so bad with intelligence! Let me give you the goddess damned—"

She'd presumably intended to say more, but he crushed his mouth down on hers before she had the chance. Her posture shifted from surprise, to anger, to passion within a few beats. One pound of the fist against his chest had given way to the familiar scratch of her fingernails as she bundled the fabric of his tunic against his chest. Briar relaxed into him, kissing him back as she melted into his intensity. Despite her weeks on the road, she still radiated chamomile and rebellion in equal proportions, though rebellion may have been the contrarian flavors of adrenaline and fury rather than anything tangible.

She broke free of the kiss first, blinking up at him with genuine confusion.

"Are you just happy to see me?"

He nuzzled into her, thwarting her attempts to ruin the moment. "Yes. Yes, I'm happy to see you, and I'm sorry for being a jackass."

She murmured a protest, but his humors were too high to entertain her angst. She attempted to half-heartedly beat her fists against his chest once or twist while objecting, but was too crushed in his hug to lose herself to rage. She'd either have to let it go or reflect on her irritation at a later date. Right now, he only had room to hold her and be grateful. Perhaps the shades of gray could come later.

Perhaps they'd never come at all.

✦

He'd expected Wren to be happy.

The fallout after he'd rushed in with the news of her arrival had been perplexing and cold in equal proportions. After leaving Briar in a bewildered state outside of her bunks, he continued picking his way down the neatly organized rows of the archers' tents, which was somewhat unusual territory for him. The spymaster had little business milling about their section of the camp, save for formal meetings. The surprised eyes he drew from enlisted troops milling about the camp confirmed the reason Briar and Wren had always opted for the privacy of his tent.

At first, Zaccai had thought Wren was simply surprised to see him among the archers given the morning they'd already shared. He'd intended to celebrate Briar's safe return. The ensuing silence sucked the air from the tent, not unlike a smothering quilt shoved over one's face. It dampened thought, emotion, and comprehension as the pair stared at each other.

"What?" Zaccai finally asked. It wasn't a particularly articulate question, but he didn't know where to start.

Wren's mouth open and closed in silent rebuke. He looked to the small table at the side of the tent, and Zaccai's followed his gaze. His eyes had landed on the empty coffee cups that he'd carried back from the commander's tent. Zaccai struggled through layers of complex emotion as he deciphered the meaning behind the captain's cryptic look.

Wren finally asked, "You're happy?"

Zaccai blinked in shock. "Of course! Aren't you?"

Wren didn't even shrug. He continued to stare wordlessly at the coffee cups, refusing to meet Zaccai's gaze.

"Wren—"

The new captain of the archers shook his head. "I'm sorry," he said quietly, "I guess I just thought we'd moved past her."

Zaccai frowned, still not comprehending. "Moved past her in what way?"

Wren closed his eyes, shoulders slumping.

"Goddess, I'm not asking you to sleep with her! She knew as well as any of us that you wouldn't be able to fraternize once you made rank. But she's still your friend and fellow officer, isn't she?" Watching Wren's face shift as he spoke helped things click into place.

Wren's eyes stayed on the empty mugs.

Realization hit Zaccai with uncomfortable weight. "Briar facilitated our meeting," he tested the words, "and once she was gone..?" He waited for Wren to meet his eyes, but the reciprocated look never came. "Wren, are you upset over primacy? Because that's not the issue here. I'm excited because I very well believed that someone I cared deeply about might have died. I thought you cared about her too. I expected us to be equally happy at her survival."

Wren nodded slowly. "Of course I'm happy that she's safe."

Zaccai still didn't understand the silence that stretched between them.

Wren chewed his lip for a moment before speaking. "I know she's how we met. I know I wouldn't have gotten the chance to be with you if it hadn't been for Bri. But...that's not what I want." Wren looked at him then, continuing, "I don't want it to be the three of us, or none of us. I thought you and I...I thought we...I thought you saw me for me." His tongue seemed to twist against his better efforts as Wren lost his words.

Zaccai felt a sudden impulse to grab Wren's hand. The urge to comfort the captain swept over him like wind whipping through autumn leaves, but it dissipated nearly as soon as it arrived. He struggled against the conflicting emotions battling for attention within the cage of his chest while he eyed the man.

"You wanted it to be us?" he asked quietly, no accusation in his tone. Zaccai prodded for Wren to meet his eyes, but the fae would not.

"Would that have been so bad? Haven't the last few weeks been..."

Zaccai took three steps to close the space between them. He caught Wren's hand. "The past few weeks have been wonderful. That doesn't mean I want Briar gone from my life. They're not mutually exclusive, Wren. The time we've spent together—"

Wren looked up at him, and he truly caught the garnet glow of the captain's eyes more than ever before. Red threads wove themselves amidst the browns, ambers, and golds in his multidimension irises. "The group dynamic isn't for me," Wren said, voice nearly a whisper. "I want it to be us."

Zaccai heard the words, but was so distantly removed from their meaning that he had to repeat the words back to ensure he'd heard them correctly. "But now that Briar's back, and you're her captain..."

"Is that so wrong? Is it so wrong that I'd want us to have

something special that has nothing to do with her? That I wouldn't want to feel like she anchors us? That I—"

Zaccai's lips tipped downward at that. He straightened his shoulders, choosing his words carefully. "Of course it's not wrong. But it's also not what she, or I, or any of us have been. We were introduced in the context of a group dynamic, and I don't think it's fair to act like I'm mistreating you for holding the original dynamic as our standard of expectation."

"It's because she's a woman, isn't it?" Wren breathed, words practically a curse.

The statement was enough to shake him from any sense of pity. Irritation flooded him as he held Wren's gaze. "What? No." His face twisted in something akin to disgust. "It's because she's always been honest about who she is and what she wants. The only time I mistrusted her was when I doubted its veracity, and I was wrong to do. I couldn't say the same of you when I met you, and I can't say the same of you now."

Finished with their exchange, Zaccai moved to leave.

Wren took a step backward, blocking the exit. "Zaccai—"

"This has nothing to do with her gender. Taking it to that place tells me how much self-awareness you lack, Wren." [CD2]

Wren's mouth opened and closed wordlessly. He looked like a panicked deer as he reached for Zaccai to stay.

Zaccai's jaw flexed as he said, "I'm not mad, Wren. I just don't think we're on the same page."

Wren blanched in near-panic as he failed to keep the pleading tone out of his otherwise-level message. "I agree. We aren't. I don't want to be someone's second choice. I don't want to be a tertiary party, or an addition, or an accessory. I want to do this with you—all or nothing."

Zaccai moved to brush past him. "Issue an ultimatum if you want," he said, "but you won't like the outcome."

"Stop." Wren flared his wings in an attempt to prevent Zaccai's escape.

"You weren't secondary," Zaccai said, fists flexing at his side. "You also aren't living in reality. Speak your truth up front so people can make informed decisions before you trick them into walking down your path. Now let me go. And please, don't revisit my tent unless you've come to apologize. And I can't speak for Bri, but, I don't recommend visiting hers either unless you're there to make it right."

PART FIVE
RELEASED

Briar's eyebrows raised as Zaccai slid across from her in the long canvas tent that served as the field's mess hall. The officers generally took their meals elsewhere, but when she was nowhere to be seen, he was pretty sure he'd find her attempting to disappear amidst the lower ranks of enlisted troops. His presence certainly turned heads. The burbling noises of scores of humans and fae engaged in conversation lulled ever so slightly at his arrival, then resumed at their typical volume.

"You make it hard to stay inconspicuous, Commander."

"Calling me by my rank? You're a poet," he teased, repeating the words she'd said to him so long ago. As he tore into his bread, he asked, "Guess what I heard?"

She set down her spoon and eyed him. "I'd hope the answer is *everything*. Isn't that your job? To know it all?"

He swallowed the mouthful and made a face, then dipped what remained of it into the stew, allowing the savory juices to soak through the stale bread. "Still mad about the volunteer thing?"

"I just don't think you make a very good spymaster. Maybe I'll put in my bid for your job." She rolled her eyes as she so often did, but there was something off about the easygoing expression he knew so well. Using her finger to clean the dredges of her bowl, she licked it clean while maintaining eye contact. "So, what did you hear?"

He flashed a white smile, saying, "You're headed back for Gwydir, Lieutenant."

"What?" Her back stiffened.

He nodded with a bit too much excitement. "They're changing out the training officers. You don't need to stay in the field. You'll be back in your bed by the end of the week."

"And you're happy about that?" She arched a brow.

He abandoned his stew, which she took as an invitation to steal. The bowl scraped against the wooden table as she dragged it toward her and began to eat the chunks of meat and carrot he'd left behind. He abandoned any hope of his meal as he continued, "Anyone would be happy to get orders out of the field!"

Her lip curled as she shrugged. "Gwydir is boring. Though I do suppose the dating pool is a little better."

"Better than six eligible lovers?"

"Yeah, Raascot's capital has to have at least...seven."

He smiled at that. "The food will also be better."

She shrugged again as she muttered, "I don't mind the food here."

Zaccai's lips tugged into the corner of his mouth. She wasn't being particularly cold, nor was she engaging like she normally did. "What's on your mind?" he finally asked.

Briar looked over her shoulder. "It's not really the best place to talk."

He extended his hand for her wrist and the moment he touched her, the sound around them disappeared. Encompassed in their protective cone of silence, no one would be able to overhear their discussion.

"Then we'll make it a good place to talk."

She narrowed her eyes, but there was no malice in the expression. "You're not great at taking hints, are you?"

"It's not my strong suit."

Briar sighed. "I spoke with Wren."

He mirrored her expression, brows gathering in the middle as he wordlessly prodded for an explanation.

"I agree, he shouldn't have given you an ultimatum."

Zaccai made no attempt to hide his surprise. "I didn't think he'd tell you."

She flipped her long, black braid over her shoulder, attempting nonchalance. "You knew as well as I that my window with him was closing. I couldn't continue to be involved in our triad based on rank alone. It was fun while it lasted, Zaccai." Her eyes dropped to what remained of the stew as her voice lowered. "It was really, *really* fun."

The air began to hiss from his lungs as if a leak had sprung. Through grit teeth, he asked, "But?"

She sighed. "I've enjoyed our time together, Cai—"

He closed his eyes slowly. He had to gather his composure before opening them. His heart descended as if twined with barbed wire as it was dropped into his stomach. He shook his head in a single denial. "Don't."

"I need to recuse myself. It's the right thing to do."

"Is this because of something Wren said? Because removing yourself from the equation isn't going to change how I feel. I don't just mean regarding how I care for you. It also won't make me forgive Wren for what he said," Zaccai pressed.

She attempted to pull her arm away from his contact, but the moment she did, his dampening would break. His large hand flexed over her forearm. He knew he held on a little too tightly, but he couldn't let her go.

"Briar, come on..."

"I'm headed back to Gwydir at the week's end anyway, right?"

"Is that what this is? Timing? I won't be in the field that much longer either, Briar. By the end of the season, I'll have my new team trained."

She pulled away again, but this time he flexed his fingers against her forearm. She glared, saying, "You're acting a little possessive, Commander. I told you what this was when we met, and you were fine with it. Don't change your tune now."

The truth of her scathing message felt a little too similar to one he'd said only a day before under very different circumstances. Trying to hold onto her felt like trying to lasso a river. But he couldn't stop himself from trying.

"Bri..."

Her tone changed to one of finality as she pushed out a sigh. "You're fae, Zaccai. This thing between you and me? This could never have been more than an affair. I couldn't—no, I *won't*—be with someone who stays young and beautiful as they watch me grow old and die. It's cruel, and I don't want it. There's nothing you can do or say to change how I feel. You are incredible, and you deserve someone who can share in that wonder for centuries. Wren should never have given you an ultimatum. I know he shouldn't have... But the two of you are well-matched. It would make me happy to see you happy, Zaccai. You deserve to be happy."

This time when she pulled away, he was too stunned to fight. The moment he let her go, the world crashed in. The onslaught of conversation, laughter, clinking utensils, and scraping chairs filled the quiet that had existed a moment prior. She gave his hand a quick squeeze, then picked up both bowls and walked across the mess hall. A human amongst a sea of wings, he watched her shape disappear amid the bodies of recruits. He stared at the space she'd left, the emptiness of her absence echoing through him.

PART SIX

TERMINATION

"Commander." The fae folded his wings and dipped his chin.

"Major," Zaccai greeted the archer and gestured for him to sit, disapproval heavy on his face. "I'd expected a report when your unit returned from the border. I didn't think I'd have to seek you out for a briefing. You've been back for days."

"My apologies." The major of the archery unit dipped his head a second time. Zaccai's bad mood was contagious in the worst way possible, and the major was clearly uncomfortable. "As it wasn't an assigned dispatch from reconnaissance, I didn't think—"

"That's exactly right. You didn't think." Zaccai kept his tone cool. "Let's see if we can change that. What did you learn at the border?"

The major knit his brows in apology. "Very little that we didn't already know, sir. The territorial dispute is over the neutral mountain range to the southwest. Farehold has pushed to absorb half of the neutral space into their territory, but if we let them expand into the neutral mountains—"

Zaccai nodded. "Then the reevers would be forced to pick a

kingdom. We've known this since the first meeting. Why did you volunteer your unit if there was no indication that there'd be new information? Why did you bring the archers for coverage if there was nothing to be gained?"

The major swallowed rather loudly. "I have every intention of taking accountability for my unit, sir, but the decision was pushed up the chain from within the unit. Our officers wanted to help, and the enlisted men below them were eager to get out of the camp and taste action. Our new captain volunteered to stay behind, and I wouldn't let my men go to the border without their leader."

Zaccai went rigid. His eye twitched as the low flames of rage flickered at the information. "Your officer rallied the enlisted archers to volunteer?"

"Yes, sir."

It was a ringing he'd heard before—one that occurred within and without. Zaccai exhaled slowly through his nose, flexing his fist against the table. Anger crawled from his stomach into his throat, following his arteries and veins to every nerve in his body. Despite the scorching heat of the impending fury, his words were icy as he asked, "Did this volunteer effort come from Wren?"

The major shifted uncomfortably. "It was a good opportunity for him to demonstrate leadership at the camp. We agreed that with his new rank—"

"Major." Zaccai stopped him through clenched teeth.
"Sir?"

"That will be all. Please return to your unit."

Zaccai knew that the major had exactly three seconds to leave the tent before he lost his temper. The man sensed the heat rolling off Zaccai like the open door of a kiln. The major nodded again as he made his eager departure.

The troops at the training camp scattered like rats as he blazed a trail through the camp. He broke through the line of tents to the archery field, all eyes turning to him as he barked a single, angry word.

"Captain!"

He ignored Briar's bewildered eyes as she froze in the midst of adjusting an archer's stance. He wasn't here for her.

Wren paled as he soaked in the vitriol emanating from him. Zaccai made no attempt to conceal how truly menacing he could be. His fighting leathers, wings flexed, jaw set, he was a force of nature, and those who had grown too comfortable with him were right to see him in his rawest form.

"Carry on," Wren choked out to the enlisted archers, but his words came out as little more than sand scattered in the wind. He swallowed, presumably in an effort to wet what Zaccai could only imagine was a panicked, dry desert in the mouth still left open in shock. Wren took ginger steps as he left the field and made his way toward Zaccai.

Zaccai didn't wait for the captain to reach him before he turned into the nearest tent. The moment Wren stepped into the darkened space, Zaccai cast his dampening over them, though he didn't need it. He would not yell. Disgust poured from every fiber of his being as he eyed the man.

"You volunteered the archers for the border so Briar would leave," he said quietly. It wasn't a question.

"If this is about Briar—" Wren attempted, face gray and shimmering with the pale sparkle of flu-like sweat.

"This is about the kind of vile monster who would manipulate a situation to get what he wanted even at the expense of the lives of others. You wanted her gone? She left. You wanted to fuck? You got what you wanted. How does it feel?"

"Zaccai—"

"Commander," he corrected with an icy chill. His rage had burned hot as he'd stormed across the camp, then dropped to the arctic, hateful temperatures known only to the bitterest winter nights.

Wren shook his head defensively, raising his hands as if to calm a snarling animal. "She's fine!" he argued. "She said herself when we spoke that she thought you and I—"

"I don't care what she said. I don't care if I ever speak to Briar again. She's not the only human who went on that mission. She's not the only vulnerable party you subjected to extreme risk. The only thing I care about is knowing that there's someone in Raascot's military—*my* military—conniving enough to send his troops to slaughter for his personal agenda."

Wren choked out a single syllable. It could have been the beginning of Cai or Commander, though no one would know. His eyes rimmed with tears as he stared at Zaccai's cold, unfeeling gaze.

"I'll leave," he said quietly.

Zaccai laughed in a furious staccato. "Leave? You don't get to leave. What you did wasn't just immoral. It wasn't just vile. It was a crime of the highest order. You'll be court-martialed. You'll be found guilty. You'll be stripped of your title, of any honor, and if I have any say in your sentence, you'll spend the next hundred years in a cell."

Wren took a step backward. His eyes widened, mouth open in a silent plea. "For wanting to be with you?"

Ice snapped as his Zaccai's emotions flared from the whiteout of a blizzard to the sizzle of an inferno, emotions within him roiling as they found no equilibrium. The fury burned through him then, temper cracking as he barked, "For attempted murder! For using Raascot's military in the single most despicable act of selfishness I've ever known! You want to be seen, Wren? You want to be known for who you are, without anyone else defining your relationship? You got your wish. The world is about to see exactly who you are."

Zaccai turned to leave, but Wren grabbed for his forearm. "It was a mistake—"

Zaccai shook his arm free, looking at the place where he'd been touched as if he'd been bitten by a snake. "Forgetting your bow is a mistake. Falling for your commander is a mistake. Manipulating a unit, deceiving your king's military—human and fae alike—at the risk of their very lives so that you can get laid is a crime. This is what you'll be known for, Wren. Congratulations. You're seen."

Zaccai dropped his dampener as he burst through the tent. Wren tried to follow, but was met by the guards who'd been stationed outside. The moment he stepped foot beyond the tent, armed men secured Wren. He called after Zaccai, but the commander didn't look back. He'd never look back again.

PART SEVEN
RETIREMENT

"Oh my goddess." Zaccai set down his drink, eyes widening. His heart skidded through his chest like a stone across still waters. The happy fiddle music, the laughter of patrons, clinking of frosted pints, and crackle of fire within the safety of its hearth dipped as he blinked against the impossible.

Gadriel turned on his bar stool and scanned the tavern to see if he could spot who or what had caught his friend's attention. The babble of noise and rush of bodies made it difficult to discern one party from the next. He looked amongst the many pressing bodies within the pub, but gave up relatively quickly, presumably neither caring nor able to distinguish much the mass of fae and humans alike. He turned back to Zaccai and raised a brow. "See someone you know?"

Zaccai nodded, standing wordlessly.

This seemed to get Gadriel's attention, as his friend set down the drink and looked up at him from where he sat at the rough-hewn counter. Zaccai meant to say something to Gadriel, but was pulled forward on instinct before finding the words. He left the table without explanation, pushing through the patrons to reach the farthest table by the window. He crossed the tavern and cautiously approached a seated couple who'd been thoroughly enjoying their pitchers.

The pair of humans halted in the midst of their conversation as he took the final tentative steps toward their table. The couple's conversation stilted as they noted his approach. The woman's eyes lit, smile flickering on her face. She reached her hand across the table and asked the burly, bearded man to get them drinks from the bar.

"Say," the man said with a friendly enough gesture, "I know you! You're the commander, are you not? I recognize you from your portrait! It's an honor. I'll be back with drinks." He assessed Zaccai with a crinkling smile and offered a clap on the arm before brushing past him to get the bartender's attention.

Zaccai barely heard the words. He swallowed down a knot and sank into the seat the man had vacated. He wasn't sure if he'd breathed once in the past five minutes.

The tavern remained merry and bustling, but he heard none of it as he stared at the woman across from him.

"I never knew you to be tongue-tied, Commander," Briar said. Her teeth still sparkled white, though the silver-gray strands of her hair now matched the shine of her teeth. The lines of her years creased the corners of her eyes, evidence of her easy smiles. She propped her chin up on one hand as she assessed him.

"Still a poet, I see," he said, voice catching in his throat. He'd meant it to be playful, but the taunt was strained. He looked over his shoulder at where the man waited at the bar. "Is that your...?"

"Husband," she finished for him. "I didn't really peg myself for motherhood, but sometimes these things sneak up on you."

Zaccai wondered if she could hear his heart over the sound of the patrons. If he didn't start inhaling and exhaling normally, she'd be forced to resuscitate him.

"I spotted you with the general. I assume military life is as exciting as ever?"

He slid his hands over the table, scooping her hand into his. She smiled sadly at the gesture, allowing her fingers to melt into the palms of his huge hands.

"I take it you don't want to talk about the good old days?" She dropped her voice to a sound barely above a whisper. Tenderness crept into her dark, lovely eyes as she looked at him.

"You're as beautiful as the day I met you," he said quietly. He was consumed by the flood of memories as they'd fallen into each other's arms, tumbling, tousling, laughing, and wringing every drop of joy from the camp that they could all those years ago. He knew it then, just as he knew it now with every fiber of his being. He would have loved her, if she had let him. "I hope your husband knows how lucky he is."

Music, laughter, and the slosh of alcohol continued battling for their attention, but their focus was only on each other. He was tempted to use their point of contact to cast a cone over them, to create a tiny bubble for the two of them alone, but it was a selfish urge. He studied her face as it softened.

She closed her eyes slowly. "He does."

Zaccai squeezed her hand, knowing if he stayed much longer, he'd fall apart. "I'm sorry," he said.

"I'm not."

And he believed her.

The threatening sting of tears pricked his eyes as he saw the years they'd spent together. He felt it all as if it were yesterday as he looked into the eyes he'd never stop loving. "After everything..."

She stopped him with a smile, sending him off with words he'd never forget. "I'll never be sorry. Not for us. We were young. We were a mess. But dammit, we had an adventure."

AFTERWORD

Remain in Gyrradin with completed *The Night and Its Moon* quartet and accompanying novellas. The villain duology, *A Chill in the Flame*, and *A Frozen Pyre* reveal the creation of the continent's demons, the origin of Uaimh Reev and the league of peacekeeping assassins, and the last fae royals of Farehold.

<u>Zaccai's story pairs well with:</u>
Inceptus *by* Arcana
chilled beer or pumpkin cider

CONTENT WARNINGS

themes of struggling with queer identity, love, loss, sexuality, group sex, tumultuous self-denial when coming out, language, betrayal, alcohol, attempted murder

THE DEER AND THE DRAGON

NO OTHER GODS

Read on for an excerpt of the urban mythology series

it was to throw them back into the water. Everything about this evening had me wishing I'd stayed in to watch the documentary about whales rather than wasting the perfume by stepping out into the world.

"What about the concert?"

I frowned, scarcely looking up from my phone. "Concert?"

Confusion faded into agitation as he studied my face. "Next week, the one I—"

Fish. Everything about this man was a fish. When they tell you that there are plenty of fish in the sea, they forget to mention that half of marine life is boring, scaly and a part of an identical school of thousands just like him. I would rather be alone, high, and looking at tropical fish next weekend. "Oh, I'm so sorry, Josh—this is my car!"

"It's Jacob."

I grimaced. I really was sorry about that one. I should have checked his name from the dating profile when I'd escaped to the restroom.

He knew the evening had soured but still had the balls to go in for a kiss. I intercepted with a side hug before launching into the street to stop my car. I closed the door and took off into the night before my date had time to recover from his wounded ego. The driver asked precisely the right number of questions, which was zero. He left me alone to the buzzing phone that illuminated the back seat of the vehicle.

(Kirby) How was the banker?
(Nia) CFO, right? Big money
(Kirby) Not like tech guy. Mar, could you call him up again?
We used to go to much nicer places when you were
sleazing it with the tech guy.
(Marlow) I'd like to sleaze it up with a loose bag of cheese
and my sweatpants
(Nia) You were supposed to get laid. How am I supposed

to live vicariously through you if you're pulling a celibacy
act
(Kirby) No, that's fair. She's always been a slut for cheese.
No one made you get married, Nia.
(Nia) And so what? I'm supposed to live with the conse-
quences of my actions?
(Marlow) I'm just going to call it an early night
(Nia) And waste a great hair and makeup day? Damn, there
must be some fantastic cheese back at your place

I clicked the button on the side of my phone, turning the screen into an obsidian mirror and leaned my head against the window, watching the black and auburn blur of homes, shadows, lawns, and fences as we crossed through a neighborhood. I used to look at houses and wonder about the lives of the people who lived inside. What did the family do to afford a home so close to downtown? What did a three-story house with fantastic landscaping cost in one of the world's flashiest cities? It had been a long time since I'd cared.

I saw the driver frown as the GPS turned into the northern part of the metropolis. It wasn't an unusual reaction. No one lived in the warehouse district. There was no reason for a girl of any repute to take a car to the warehouses in high heels and red lipstick. He pulled up along the sidewalk and eyed what had once been a bread factory. His expression deepened into worry at the smattering of lights and darkened entryway.

"Is this right, miss?"

"Home sweet home." I smiled. I flashed him my screen to show the glowing rating I'd sent his way as I slid out of the car. His eyebrows remained knit, but he shrugged as I closed the door. He wasn't paid enough to care.

A blanket-like quiet pressed in as the car pulled away—a sound challenging to achieve anywhere in the city. There was no traffic, no pedestrians, no indication that anyone but the phantoms of long-dead industry tycoons haunted these corridors. The April night clung to the last of spring's chill, sending goose bumps up and down my bare legs. I fished a metallic rose-gold card from my purse and pressed it against the panel, satisfied when it buzzed.

I rounded the brick corridor for the atrium, where an ever-attentive receptionist waited to respectfully greet me. She was one of four and arguably my favorite. No matter how short my skirt, how high my heels, or how late the hour, she remained polite without speaking. I knew her boyfriend's name, I gave her chocolates every holiday, and we never failed to gush about the new episodes of *Fires and Swords* if I loitered in the hallway, but she had an innate gift for knowing when I was overwhelmed and needed silence. Perhaps intuition was a prerequisite for anyone who took a job in luxury apartments.

Though she'd never say it outright, her expressions conveyed the same long-standing concern that I'd stumbled through the door after too many dates to count. She'd helped me get into the building when I was a bit too drunk to see my phone and buzzed me up to my room whenever I'd lost too much brain function to recall how my card worked. It seemed like a safe bet that she was not the sort of person who got high at aquariums.

The small bank of polished elevators waited quietly, all in disuse given the lateness of the hour. One opened for me the moment I pressed the button.

I didn't wait for the elevator doors to close before slipping out of my heels, dangling the sharpened ends from one hand. I caught the brief, disapproving narrowing of eyes through the rapidly closing doors and flashed my most dazzling smile. Part of me respected her bravery. It was bold to be judgmental of the residents when they knew precisely how much these apart-ments cost.

I pressed the glittery, metallic card onto the pad to gain access to my floor—second from the top. The penthouse hadn't been available, and I'd been okay with it. Everyone who lived here had their reasons for wanting to stay off the world's radar, and there wasn't a better establishment in the city for those with deep enough pockets to erase themselves from the map. The building's discretion had been worth the downgrade, and as someone who lived alone, I couldn't have justified the extra space unless I was looking to install a private bowling alley.

The elevator door opened noiselessly onto my floor. There were thirteen units in the entire building—two per floor, save for the lucky bastard who'd snagged the thirteenth. I walked barefoot down the sparkling black marble to my room and pressed my thumb into the pad, allowing it to scan my fingerprint until a subtle click told me the mechanisms had unlocked.

It was dark in my apartment and stayed that way. I'd had the features for automatic lights disabled the day I'd moved in.

I tossed my purse onto the floor, leaving it in a jumble with my shoes. I walked to the window and stared out over the twinkling lights of the city and the sliver of river I could spot from my unit. I was a sucker for a good view.

The hairs on the back of my neck prickled in the way they did when one knew they were being watched. The rush of gin, moss, and mist filled the room the moment before I heard it. I breathed it in like a prayer.

"Leave it open" came a male voice from the shadows.

I fought the deep, conflicting bloom that emanated from somewhere near my center. My toes curled, heart thundering at the purr of his voice. "Don't do this to me," I grumbled halfheartedly, but I was certain he heard the ghost of a smile in my voice.

"Didn't go well?" he asked.

I continued facing the window but reached over my head for the zipper. Years had gone by, and I was still breathless every time he spoke. It was so easy to lose my resolve whenever those silken words tumbled over his lips. I managed to give the thin metal a tug but lost my grip on it as I said, "He was utterly forgettable."

"They all will be," he said, brushing my hair away from my neck. Goose bumps started at the nape of my neck and slithered down my spine. He held the top of my dress in one strong hand, using the other to gently tug the zipper. He stopped before releasing it more than a quarter of an inch. I waited for the next sensation, but nothing came. Tension swelled as I swallowed another deep breath of earth and perfume.

"What?" I breathed.

The electric current of his touch coursed through me.

"Holy fuck," I murmured, falling to pieces.

His fingers began to work their way up the hem of my dress, nudging it up over my hips. My stomach clenched. My lips parted in a stifled gasp, eyes closing as he came up behind me. His mouth sucked gently on the tender place where my throat met my shoulder. Every sense in my body homed in on the delicious sensation. His mouth moved to the back of my neck, hands dropping from my hips to urge me forward. I leaned into the floor-to-ceiling glass, letting the cold seep into me as his hand slid from my inner thigh, higher, *higher*.

"Oh god," I gasped when he grazed the soaked evidence of my black-lace panties.

"You know better than that," he chided softly at my choice in words, a teasing warmth in his voice. He relaxed his body into mine until I was pressed wholly against the window. "Now, are you going to let me in?"

My face betrayed the battle going on in my head and heart. My body ached for him. My breasts peaked against the thin dress. The pulsing in my chest extended into every piece of me, and I felt my heartbeat in my greediest places. My fingers clenched against the glass. He chuckled lightly.

"Nothing without your permission," he said, fingers still grazing me with tantalizing slowness. The tingle of the water between my legs trickling onto my inner thighs elicited a low groan of approval. His fingers continued to move over the thin fabric.

I gasped against the sensation, and he leaned into my throat once more, smiling through my pleasure.

"You know I'm…" Words felt useless.

"You're what?" he pressed me into the window with more force.

"I'm trying to stop."

His fingers quickened as he said, "As if I don't know you, Love. We both know it'll never make you happy. But if you'd prefer mundane restaurants and forgettable men over what I can offer you…" His hand stilled.

My lust, my greed, my denial came out in a single, short sound. My eyes opened as I turned back to the shadows, but I knew what I'd see before I turned.

Despite the bandage-tight dress around my hips and the puddle of evidence on my legs, I knew he wasn't there. He hadn't been there in a long, long time.

THE DEER AND THE DRAGON
NO OTHER GODS

This new series from Piper CJ is the start of an urban fantasy based on the real world. As war looms, it's a fight for survival, a pantheon of deities and a belief in love, all working together to build an epic narrative.

"HOW DOES A HUMAN GIRL LOSE THE PRINCE OF HELL?"

Marlow needs to believe she's crazy. The alternative would mean embracing the gift—or curse—shared by her mother and grandmother: she can see angels and demons, including a dark and haunting entity who's been with Marlow her entire life. At least, she believes that's all he is until a fae from the Nordic pantheon strolls into her life and informs her that she's been sharing a bed with the Prince of Hell.

A Prince who's now gone *missing*.

Before she knows it, Marlow is deeply entangled in a centuries-old war, stumbling straight into a battleground between mighty beings of myth and legend from powerful pantheons around the world. And who will come out on top may just depend on her and the love she never dared to believe in.

FOR FANS OF:
- Romantasy
- Mythology & folklore
- Kickbutt heroines
- Fae, angels, and demons
- Hilarious banter
- *Hazbin Hotel*

ABOUT THE AUTHOR

Piper CJ, author of the USA Today bisexual fantasy series *The Night and Its Moon,* urban mythology series *No Other Gods,* and New York Times bestselling series *Fern's School for Wayward Fae,* is a photographer, hobby linguist, and French fry enthusiast. She has an M.A. in Folklore and a B.A. in Broadcasting, which she used in her former life as a morning-show weather girl, hockey podcaster, and in audio documentary work. Now when she isn't playing with her dog, she's gaming, binging cartoons, dissecting fairy tales, or disappointing her parents.

website: pipercj.com

instagram.com/piper_cj
tiktok.com/pipercj